COVENTRY SCHOOLS LIBRARY SERVICE

Please return this book on or before
last date stamped.

Coventry City Council

D0493289

ReadZone Books Limited

50 Godfrey Avenue
Twickenham
TW2 7PF
UK

Coventry Education & Learning Service	
3 8002 01793 730 3	
Askews & Holts	16-Jun-2015
	£6.99

© ReadZone Books 2014
© in text Anna Wilson 2005
© in illustrations Mike Gordon 2004

Anna Wilson has asserted her right under the Copyright Designs and Patents Act 1988
to be identified as the author of this work.

Mike Gordon has asserted his right under the Copyright Designs and Patents Act 1988
to be identified as the illustrator of this work.

First published in this edition by Evans Brothers Ltd, London in 2010.

Every attempt has been made by the Publisher to secure appropriate permissions for material
reproduced in this book. If there has been any oversight we will be happy to rectify the situation
in future editions or reprints. Written submissions should be made to the Publisher.

British Library Cataloguing in Publication Data (CIP) is available for this title.

Printed and bound in China for Imago

All rights reserved. No part of this publication may be reproduced, stored in a retrieval system
or transmitted, in any form or by any means, electronic, mechanical, photocopying, recording
or otherwise, without the prior permission of ReadZone Books Limited.

ISBN 978 1 78322 450 0

Visit our website: www.readzonebooks.com

Terry the Flying Turtle

by Anna Wilson

illustrated by Mike Gordon

"I'm clever," said Terry the Turtle. Polly the Chimp laughed.

Terry was cross.

"I **am** clever," said Terry.

"I can fly."

Polly laughed and laughed.
"You can't fly!" she said.

Terry was cross.
"I **can** fly," he said.
"You'll see."

"Will you help me?"
Terry asked the parrot.
"I want to fly."

The parrot laughed.
Terry was cross.
"Please will
you help me?"
he asked.

"All right," said the parrot.
"Hold this twig and I'll
hold it too."

"Why?" asked Terry.

"Because it will help you fly," said the parrot.

The parrot held on.
Terry held on.

The parrot flew.
Terry flew!

The animals watched.
"Look at Terry!" they said.
"He looks silly!"

Terry was cross.
"I'm not silly," he shouted.
"You're silly. I'm flying!"

Terry fell down
and down.

SPLASH!

"You look silly now!" Polly said.

3 8002 01793 730 3